S0-ABB-285

The Turtle and the Moon

by Charles Turner

illustrated by Melissa Bay Mathis

DUTTON CHILDREN'S BOOKS NEW YORK

For Jonathan, Curt, and Kathryn
C. T.

For my brother John, whose presence in my life
makes all the difference
M. B. M.

Text copyright © 1991 by Charles Turner
Illustrations copyright 1991 © by Melissa Bay Mathis
All rights reserved.

Library of Congress Cataloging-in-Publication Data

Turner, Charles (Charles E.), 1930—
The turtle and the moon/by Charles Turner;
illustrated by Melissa Bay Mathis.—1st ed.
p.   cm.
Summary: A lonely turtle makes friends with the moon.
ISBN 0-525-44659-1
[1. Turtles—Fiction.   2. Moon—Fiction.]
I. Mathis, Melissa Bay, ill.   II. Title.
PZ7.T85428Tu   1991
[E]—dc20   90-43841 CIP AC

Published in the United States by Dutton Children's Books,
a division of Penguin Books USA Inc.

Designer: Riki Levinson

Printed in Hong Kong by South China Printing Co.
First Edition   10 9 8 7 6 5 4 3 2 1

The turtle lived alone
in the tall grass beside the lake.

Every day he went for a walk
and then he took a nap,

and then he dived into the water
and went for a swim.

Then he took a sunbath

and went for another swim.

Sometimes the turtle got lonely
because there was nobody to play with.

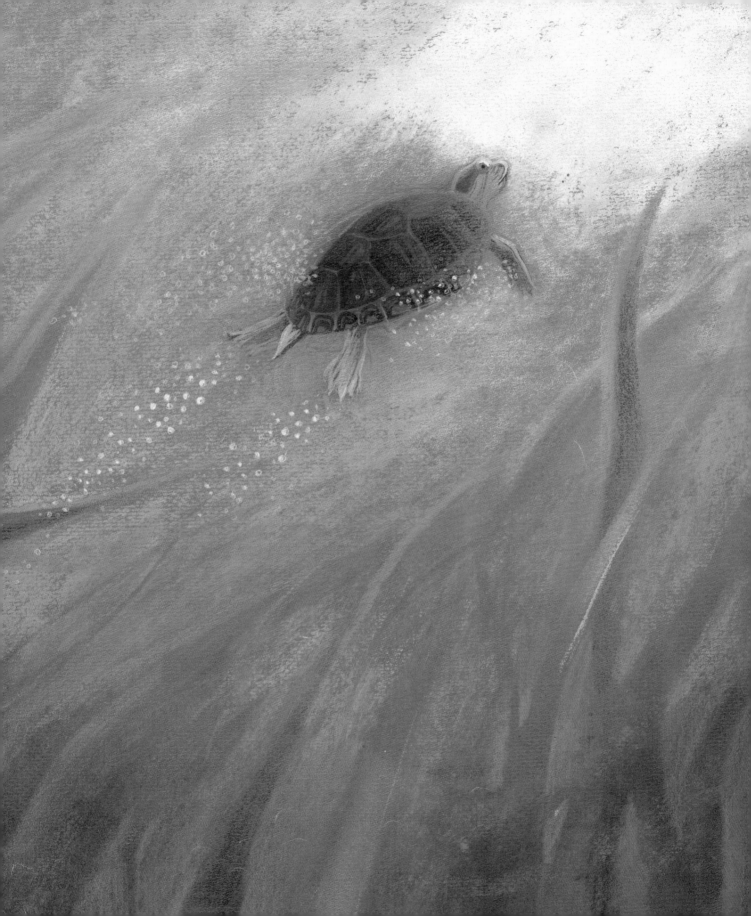

At the end of the day,
even before the sun went down,
the turtle would draw himself into his shell
and go to sleep.

But one restless night he woke up
and poked his head out
and saw something so big
and so round and so strange
that he snapped at it.

The moon—for that was what it was—slid behind a cloud.
"I'm sorry I frightened you," the turtle said.
"Come out and I promise not to snap at you again."
But the moon did not come out.
"Come out and let's go for a swim," the turtle said.

"I bet you *can't* swim," the turtle scoffed.
And then the moon peeped out.
"I'll race you," the turtle challenged,
   and he turned and lumbered toward the lake

But when he poked his nose through the tall grass,
the turtle was surprised.
The moon was already in the water, waiting for him.

The turtle threw himself into the shining lake
—plop!—

and suddenly the moon was splashing around,
playing hide-and-seek and tag,
diving down here,
bobbing up there,
shimmering in every direction.

"Show-off," the turtle said,
   and he began to show off too,
   swimming in circles,
   ducking his head,
   kicking up his heels.

When the sun edged the horizon,
the turtle and the moon were very tired and very sleepy.
The turtle drew himself into his shell and slept.
The fading moon drifted to the other side of the lake,

Not a trace of it was left when the turtle woke up.
The turtle went for a walk as usual,
and then he took a nap as usual,

and then he dived into the water and went for a swim
and took a sunbath and went for another swim,
as usual.

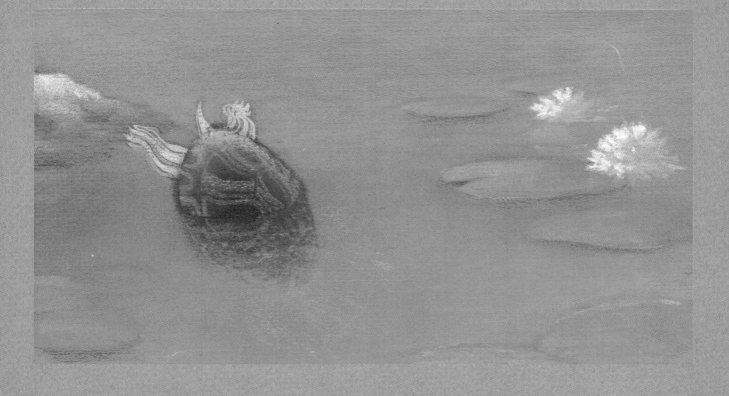

But that evening the turtle did *not* go to bed
before dark, as usual.
That evening, he waited for the sun to go down,
for night to fall,

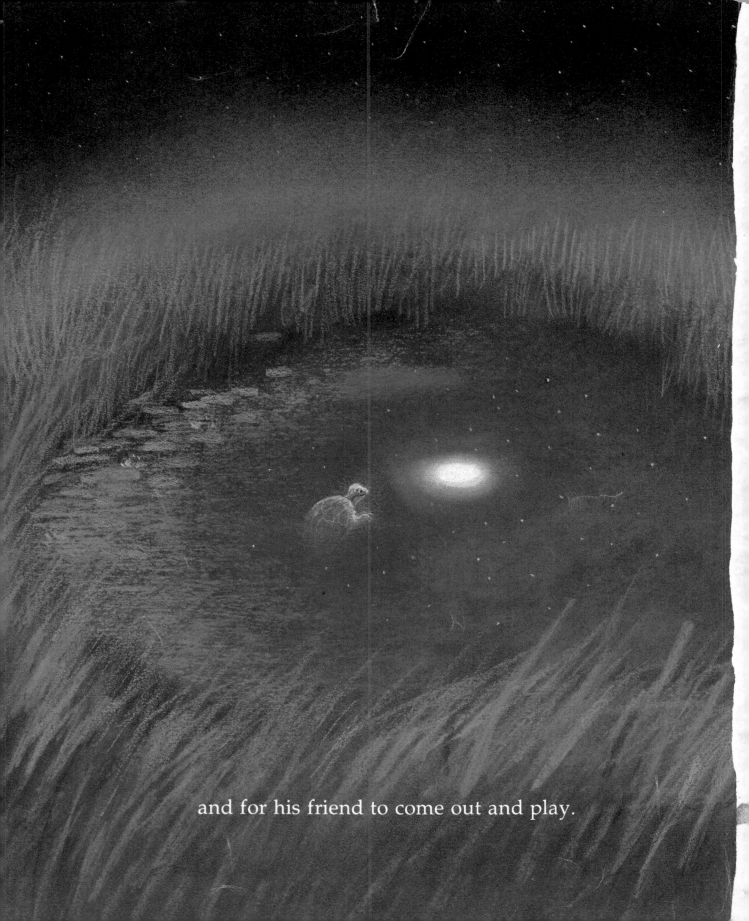

and for his friend to come out and play.

LINDEN PUBLIC LIBRARY

a 3950400038949 0b

38949

Ja
Turner
The turtle and the moon

9/92

14.95

1997
FEB 2 1 1997
97   95
97
EP 98
NOV
APR 98
JUL 98
1993

LINDEN FREE PUBLIC LIBRARY
31 EAST HENRY STREET
LINDEN, NEW JERSEY

1993
1993
1993
1993